Escapades of a
BELLY DANCER

Volume 2

THE BOOK OF DAVE

ONLINE DATING
GONE BAD

BELLE SOUTH

BelleSouth.Club

Acknowledgements

Thanks to all the online dating services! I've had some unusual experiences, some good, some not so good, some downright rude.

I want to acknowledge the Women's Prosperity Network and the founders, Nancy Matthews, Trish Carr and Susan Weiner. They have created an International network of entrepreneurs in a safe space for acquiring knowledge, training, networking and practice of the skills we develop as members of the Women's Prosperity Network. My books would not have been published if not for this extraordinary group of women and the supportive environment they have created. Thank you ladies!!

Thanks to Candi Parker of Parker House Publishing for your guidance and professionalism. Thanks to Judee Light for editing my work and introducing me to Women's Prosperity Network. These two amazing women have shared in one of my finest accomplishments, during the best time of my life.

Thanks to Allison Ronis! Not only for your endless patience, effortless and tireless technical support, but also for your loving friendship, creativity and advice.

To all the men that I met online, thank you for the experience, whether it was good or bad. I've enjoyed the chase, being chased, writing to you, receiving messages from you, meeting you and even dating some of you. And thanks to my friends for sharing your stories with me about your experiences.

Thanks to my mom for every dance class she took me to and the piano lessons that taught me the rhythm I use for dancing and drumming. And life. As a child, we lived at the beach every summer in New York. I love the beach; it is my safe spot. I also learned to garden from my mom, the beginning of my affinity for the Earth and Nature.

Thanks to my dearest friends in Wakulla County, Judy Grass, Nickey Lepp, Tammie Nason, Brian Martin, Jeremy Miller, Stephen Smart, and to my little sister Elise David, whose support, friendship and love has carried me through my most difficult times. I love you all.

Introduction

In Volume One of *Escapades of a Belly Dancer, The Empath*, Gillian has an amazing relationship (or what she thought was a relationship) with Will. Divorced for almost two years, Gillian relocated to Robertsville, Florida for a wonderful position as bank president of Robertsville Savings and Loan. Her real estate broker and dear friend, Sylvester Morland, had helped her find the most beautiful place she had ever lived on some acreage just north of Tallahassee. Gillian's two sweet and loving dogs had room to run and the longer she lived there, the more critters Gillian saw gathering on her property.

In Volume Two, *The Book of Dave, Online Dating Gone Bad*, in a very short period of time, Gillian falls in love with a man that does not exist. Knowing Internet dating was a fifty-fifty proposition, that if it was too good to be true, it wasn't. The end result was that of the satisfaction of a needed distraction from her last relationship.

Coming soon ~ In Volume Three, *A Weekend with Ali,* Gillian has an experiential relationship with another woman who recently moved to town. Gillian's love interest, Glenn, is out of the country and they share stories about their respective adventures until his return. Ali becomes part of their social circle and influences the way Gillian feels about her monogamous orientation.

About the Author

Belle South was born in New York and raised in Los Angeles with two sisters, one older and one younger. At the age of three, she tagged along to her elder sister's dance classes and danced throughout most of her adolescence, in the classical dances of ballet, jazz, tap and acrobatics. In high school Belle studied Modern Dance and began a process of self-actualization. Once in college, after two years of Psychology and Sociology majors, Belle went back to the Arts and took up Modern Ballet, Modern Jazz and Afro-Cuban Ethnic Dance.

At the age of twenty-three, Belle sold everything she owned and moved to Kauai to live off the land. When she returned to the mainland, she met her first husband and took up Belly Dancing. Her Belly Dance teacher was mesmerizing; her femininity and grace, the dark eye make-up, the sensuous movement, the costuming and the community belly dancing builds amongst women. Belle was hooked!

Belle went on to become a certified Belly Dance instructor after studying with over seventy-five teachers, exploring a variety of styles from many countries, and she then created her own belly dance theory in her fifties. After hearing too many women say they were too old or too fat to belly dance, she pointed out that she herself was over fifty and overweight and shared that the ecstasy of belly dance has nothing to do with age or size.

If you would like to know more about sensuality, Qigong or belly dancing, visit www.YourPathwayToPleasure.com. There you will find tools to feel your sensuality soar in new ways; download *Ten Tantric Tips in a Snap!*

To contact Belle, write her at Belle@BelleSouth.Club.

TABLE OF CONTENTS

CHAPTER ONE

After the Phone Call

Gillian hung up the phone after two hours of speaking to Duke Lawrence. Duke was the first empath Gillian had ever known. He was a very sensuous man and she could not keep her hands off him when they first met. He had come back suddenly and quite unexpectedly into her life after twenty-some-odd years saying how he thought of her every single day over those years. Gillian was surprised that she had made that kind of impact on a man, so long ago. Duke told her he thought of her every day of his marriage. He'd been trying to find Gillian since his divorce and he was confident that they were destined to be together. The sexual bond they'd had trumped all of his sexual partners put together. He said she was the perfect woman, completely feminine and he loved her spark. She was the love of his life. Duke wanted to grocery shop together and cook together, he thought it was sexy. Duke said all the right things about commitment, love, marriage and fidelity. He said that he was hopeful, exhilarated and dying to see her. They talked about meeting up and seeing if there was anything left of their original attraction to each other from their days at Will Rogers State Park and their instant connection. When they were saying goodbye, Duke said, "I love you Gillian," and she was momentarily dazed by his expression. They primarily communicated with emails, as their three-hour time difference made it complicated to call. Duke wrote Gillian the most heartfelt messages. They were like love letters and tugged at Gillian's heart. He continued to say that he considered her "the one that got away." He thanked her for teaching him how to make love to a woman when they first met and lived together for a short time.

Duke was living in California. He'd gotten married, had a son and was recently divorced after a twenty-five year marriage. Gillian believed it broke his heart and now he was looking for the perfect forever relationship. Arrangements were made to meet after a month of getting reacquainted over the phone. Duke flew into the Tallahassee Airport on a

Friday afternoon to spend a long weekend with Gillian. Neither one of them knew exactly what to expect when Duke got off the plane and exited towards Baggage Claim. Gillian was waiting as close to his exit as she could. There was no mistaking him as he walked quickly towards her, dropped his carry-on bags, took her into his arms and gave her an amazingly long, deep kiss in front of everyone in Baggage Claim.

Gillian was flooded with a fever of feelings, immersing herself into Duke's kiss while trying to ignore the many folks watching their reunion. She felt a bit uncomfortable but allowed herself the experience. Duke looked relatively the same, except his red hair and red beard had gone gray. They gathered up Duke's bags and walked to Gillian's car. Being the directionally challenged woman that she was, Gillian programmed her navigation system to guide them to St. George Island where a cottage on the beach was rented for the weekend. The beach had always been Gillian's favorite place; her Scorpio tendencies drove her to the water in search of peace and tranquility. What better place to get reacquainted with an old love.

Diane, Gillian's secretary, was pet sitting at

Gillian's, taking care of the gardens and having the ability to stay in what everyone who visited decided to call Sanctuary. Ever since the first time Sylvester Morland, her Realtor, brought her to her home, being there was like visiting a sanctuary. Time stood still. Experiences were transformational. Relationships went to another level. With all the stresses, politics and violence in the world, one could visit Gillian to find their "mellow yellow", as Sylvester called it. Not wanting to disrupt that special feeling at home, Gillian thought it best to reunite with Duke on neutral ground, somewhere they had never been together before. At the beach, they would be faced with quiet time and few interruptions.

The ride to St. George Island was filled with conversation. Duke talked about his work in Virginia as a TV director for the Senate committee meetings. He had moved back to California when his mom was ill. After she died, he then split his time between Virginia and California. He spoke of his son, Barry, who was now twenty-five and finding his way. Much of the conversation revolved around Duke's marriage and ultimate divorce. Gillian considered the fact that Duke had some unresolved issues about his ex-wife and was bitter about the way it ended. She hoped not to hear about his marriage all weekend. She yearned for some one-on-one attention.

Their beach cottage was ready when they arrived. It was such a beautiful day. The first thing Gillian did was run to the water's edge and absorb the clean, cool, fresh smelling air of the sea. As they unloaded their luggage to bring it inside, Duke took Gillian in his arms, looked deeply into her eyes and thanked her for giving them the opportunity to reconnect. He gave her another very long kiss on the patio facing the Gulf of Mexico. Old feelings came to the surface and once there was nothing standing between them and the bedroom, Duke's hands caressed Gillian's body from the top of her head to her bottom as he ushered her onto the bed. Their clothes were off in moments, and the old familiar feeling of not being able to keep their hands off each other returned.

Quite unexpectedly, Duke went directly to Gillian's thighs with his tongue. He said he wanted to taste her again and drive her crazy. Duke was relentless; he held Gillian down and kept giving her head until the bed was soaked with her pleasure. She basically had to beg him to stop and allow her a turn of putting her mouth on his body. It must have been an hour before Duke put his love inside Gillian. After cleaning up and fixing her hair, changing into a very short, white sundress and beige sandals, Gillian took Duke to dinner in Apalachicola. They ate delicious steamed oysters on the water while drinking Long Island Iced Teas and watched the sun go down. The first day had gone well.

A storm came in early in the morning of their second day together. There was no rush to get out of bed so they made the most of their time in bed. Duke would pleasure Gillian with his mouth until she could take no more, then he would have his way with her and enjoy his release. Afterwards, Duke made some coffee and they drank it out on the covered porch, watching the gentle rainfall. Gillian spoke about the relationship of the tide and the moon, the storm and the surf, just making conversation. Duke disagreed with everything she said, stating that he knew some lifeguards in California who told him there was no relationship to any of it. Gillian thought it odd that Duke would argue about something like that, and disagree with so many things. She wondered if this was a control thing. She thought back to when they were younger and why it didn't work out. Duke was a control freak, a Virgo, with an extremely strong personality. He should have understood that he would never be able to boss Gillian around. She was a very strong Scorpio woman with a mind of her own.

All day Saturday and Sunday Duke wanted to talk about Will, the man who was Gillian's last relationship. Gillian said that their time together was about the two of them, not Will. As many times as he brought up Will, Gillian told him that subject was off limits and she didn't want to talk about it with him. Gillian felt that Duke ruined their weekend together by not shutting up about Will. Yes, Duke was an insistent control freak.

Their sensual connection was still there, the sex was very pleasurable and they would have sex three times in a day. When they were not having sex, it seemed to Gillian that Duke was the kind of person that always had to be right. By Sunday, when preparing to return back to the Tallahassee airport, they were feeling satiated. In her car, Duke asked Gillian how he thought their reunion went. She said, "I think it

7

was caustic." Duke said, "That's not good!" And no it wasn't. Gillian hated arguing and regardless of how good sex can be it's not worth being aggravated the rest of the time she spent being involved with someone. She'd had enough aggravation over Will to not want to go there again.

As Gillian dropped Duke off at the airport, they kissed goodbye and knew they would be in touch with each other. Driving back home, thoughts of Will came back to Gillian. She remembered how sensuous their physical relationship had been and how difficult it would be to ever find another whose energy was so strong and so magnetic. Darn him! It had been over a month since they spoke.

Duke and Gillian continued with their long distance relationship and talking about their feelings for each other. And while they did love each other, there were some pretty big obstacles between them, besides his being a control freak. Turned out that Duke hated Florida and wanted to live a bi-coastal life between Virginia and California. Gillian had acclimated to the Florida weather and absolutely loved her space. Many times during their hour-long conversations, Duke would challenge what Gillian said, strongly disagreeing with her. It got old and Gillian tired of their disagreements during each call. Duke didn't seem to have the time to visit her while he renovated the old home in California, and Gillian had no desire to leave home.

CHAPTER TWO

What Happened to Will?

Will's flight from Tallahassee to California was pleasantly uneventful, just the way he liked it. He knew that his old high school flame, Ashling, might be involved with this new government program and the thought of seeing her again made him tingle inside. When Will arrived at the Los Angeles airport he was delightfully surprised to see Ashling there to pick him up. Her beauty had not declined with age and he felt the same attraction to her as when they were in high school, on prom night and during their first time making love. Conversation came easily for them on their long ride to the facility and Ashling felt safe as she confided in Will about her unhappiness in her marriage. Because she had two young children she wasn't sure about staying in a loveless marriage or getting a divorce. Her husband was gone for long periods of time as a truck driver and they had been sleeping in separate rooms for the past six months.

Will kept the focus of the conversation on Ashling and never mentioned his relationship with Gillian. Will realized that Ashling was flirting with him a little and old feelings came flooding back to him about their youth and earlier attraction. Ashling was the first redhead Will had ever been with and he liked the way the carpet matched the drapes, the only way to tell a natural redhead. Ashling was a natural redhead and her beautiful green eyes still sparkled as she spoke. Will found himself confused about his feelings for Gillian and his current vulnerability to Ashling. He could smell her perfume, her hair and her breath inside the little car they were driving in.

It was a bit of a ride from the airport to the government site selected for the organic medical marijuana greenhouse contract Will was working on. He was excited about the project as a firm believer in the medicinal benefits of marijuana as a replacement for pharmaceutical drugs given to veterans suffering from post-traumatic stress disorder and cancer patient relief. Research was being done using the plant-based healing properties to treat autism and depression. Will's interest

11

in the environment and organic processes supported his overall interest in the project.

By the time Ashling pulled into the parking lot for the project they nicknamed "Going Green" Will knew in his heart he would be with Ashling again, soon. She had not entered his mind for years and he had no idea whatsoever that he would see her again, let alone become involved with her again. His mind wandered to how her body would feel, if she tasted the same, if she would respond to his body the way she once did. It was becoming increasingly difficult to keep his body from reacting to his thoughts. Will was really happy to arrive at the site and get to work, to put some distance between himself and Ashling.

Their first day went quickly with all the details of a new project coming together. The requests for proposals were all in, the government funds were in a local bank for easy access, and as luck would have it, Ashling was the purchasing agent for the project and Will would be seeing a lot of her. At the end of their first day, Ashling drove Will into town for some dinner. After a quick tour of the town center, at Will's request, she swung by the liquor store for some alcoholic beverages and then drove Will over to where he was staying in a nearby Bed and Breakfast. Will was pleased with the small cottage building behind the owner's home where he would stay for the duration of his time working in California. The owner of the Bed and Breakfast was absent; Will had all the privacy in the world. There were bricks on the ground, there was a small deck, and it was a lovely, private space surrounded by a lush garden. In the most natural way, Will invited Ashling inside his cottage room for a nightcap. Happy to receive the invitation, Ashling gave Will a look of happiness and love. They unloaded her car, putting Will's luggage inside the cottage, grabbed a couple of glasses with ice and made a couple of vodka drinks.

As they relaxed on the two chairs on the deck, sipping on their cocktails, sharing memories of high school, they both felt a desire to be closer to each other. Will leaned over from his chair and gently kissed Ashling on the lips. That kiss was the beginning of an affair to be remembered. That one kiss got them up out of their chairs, lips locked together, finding their way into the cottage and onto the bed that was in the center of the room. It was a heavenly feeling, a spiritually deep connection that still existed between them. Almost unknowingly, they quickly undressed each other and found themselves in a bubble of love. The desire, the urgency, the memories consumed them for two hours. Will explored his past love's body with new knowledge, pleasured her with techniques he learned over time and enjoyed hearing her moan as she came.

Ashling was overcome with pleasure. Her husband had never been the best lover and although she was in love with him at the time of their marriage, and for the birth of their children, something had shifted over the last year and the romantic love was gone. They hadn't been intimate for over six months so she was really ready for some good lovin'. And who better than Will to fill that need. He was still beautiful. His football days served him very well; he was built like a rock, and, no doubt, still well endowed, not to mention the perfect gentleman. Ashling remembered his taste and was happy to taste him again. They had both learned a few new tricks since high school. Their time together reuniting felt right in every way.

A whole week went by before Will could even *think* of contacting Gillian. What was he going to tell Gillian? Will didn't have a clue what he would say, how he would say anything or how he really felt about her. Will was too nervous to even think about speaking to her, let alone actually speaking to her. He had no idea how she would feel or react and decided he could not stand the thought of having this kind of conversation with her. Will went underground and immersed himself in his work and did not call her.

In a way Will was embarrassed to speak with Gillian. What would he say? He was so overwhelmed by Ashling's reappearance in his life, and the effect she had on him, that he was unclear about the direction to take. His relationship with Gillian was the most sensuous relationship he had ever experienced. Gillian reached him at a different level. Physically speaking, it was off the charts. The contrast of his feelings between the two women gave him a headache.

For the past month, Will felt a profound love for Ashling. When they made love, Will wanted to devour Ashling as if he would never get enough. He felt a total connection between body, mind, heart and soul and hoped Ashling felt it too. It was as if they were each other's first truly intimate lovers, and in fact they were, on Prom night. It was when Will realized his strong feelings for Ashling that he decided it was time to call Gillian. He waited until the end of his workday, knowing Gillian was done with work since it was three hours later, and called Gillian in Florida. The conversation was a short one. Will asked that they take some time off from each other so he could explore his feelings for Ashling. Gillian said that was not a problem. Regardless of her previous feelings for Will, Gillian didn't appreciate the disrespectful way Will had treated her and was thoroughly disappointed with his behavior. Gillian was done with Will and his inconsideration. Gillian thought how synchronistic it was that Duke had appeared in her life just as Ashling had appeared in Will's.

From that point forward, Gillian decided to focus on her work at the bank and getting Scott Sanders the loan he needed to open his dive shop. She was very excited about this new project, there were many details involved in planning progress payments of funds for the property, construction, stocking of inventory and decorating Scott's new business. Now that Sylvester's Boxwood Bar and Grill was up and running successfully, and the progress payments towards the loan were being made on time, Gillian had another fun project to help develop. Moving to Florida had been a great choice overall and Gillian had no regrets. She loved her work and the people she came in contact with as bank President. Robertsville was a small southern town and Gillian was from the big city of Los Angeles. It took a little while to adapt to the slower pace, the heat and humidity, different political views and the social climate. As an empath, she felt quite calmed by the quiet and nature surrounding her. Gillian was able to slow down and enjoy feeling vulnerable in nature. She was safe and happy.

CHAPTER THREE

Let's Go Online!

A short time later, after feeling a profound feeling of emptiness, Gillian decided to give online dating a try. Her secretary, Diane, had met a wonderful sixty-year-old man named Marv that lived in Montana on a forty-acre ranch. He seemed almost too good to be true. He would fly Diane in for a week at a time and if Gillian got too busy without her secretary, the bank would call in a temporary assistant. Gillian was a strong believer in being able to live your personal life and allowed Diane the time off, without pay, to explore what life has to offer. It also strengthened her relationship with her employee as they shifted into a wonderful friendship.

Gillian had been married most of her adult life. She was enjoying her newfound freedom. The weekend she spent with Duke proved to be flattering and sexually satisfying, but she didn't see any kind of future with his being such a control freak. And since Will had removed himself from her life, Gillian realized how much she missed their physical relationship and decided to join an online dating site. Robertsville was a very small town and there weren't too many prospects locally. One evening after work Gillian fixed herself a shot of sipping tequila and went to a popular site for casual dating.

Diane sent a link to Gillian to join the online dating site she used to meet her beau. Gillian developed a profile, calling herself Savannah Scorpio, checking the box "divorced". What was she looking for? She checked the boxes of casual sex, short-term relationship and long-term relationship. Was she female, male, straight, gay or bisexual? What she didn't realize is in checking all these boxes, she accidentally checked bisexual. Gillian answered at least one hundred questions about life, relationships and sex. She selected a few recent photos, posted them and waited. The next morning there were twenty messages! Gillian felt encouraged that she might actually meet someone. The one man that caught her eye was Dave. Dave was South African, a white man, sixty years old, with bulging muscles in his short-sleeved t-shirt, a flat belly, in tight jeans, leaning on a tree. It had to have been a professionally done photo. He was gorgeous and older, probably more mature than the men Gillian had recently been spending her time with. Dave owned his own construction company and had just finished negotiating a construction contract in West Africa.

After numerous emails back and forth for a week, Gillian gave Dave her phone number and told him her real name. Dave said the sweetest things. He wanted to make Gillian his Queen. He said he would love her with all his heart. He texted several times a day and it made Gillian feel desirable again. Dave called one morning; he had to fly through Orlando and asked Gillian to meet him at the airport. Gillian couldn't make it but she found herself longing to meet Dave. Maybe she would be able to meet him on his way back from West Africa. The fantasy of Dave was very exciting. Gillian imagined what he would look like naked. In the photo, his hands looked proportionate, if not large, for his body, a good sign. There were nights when Gillian could not fall asleep. She would fantasize about kissing Dave, how his tongue would feel inside her mouth, running down her body, between her thighs. She could imagine his face above hers as she lay in bed. It was almost as if he were there making her feel the orgasms she would have. Sleep then came easily and was filled with wonderful dreams for her future.

The phone calls continued for two more weeks. Dave professed his love and desire for meeting Gillian and making her his wife, his Queen. It was a whirlwind romance; he was already talking about marriage. He had no problem moving to Florida, he could work anywhere. Gillian's heart was healing. She felt love for a man she had never met. Was it real? Was she just feeling vulnerable? Each day was filled with anticipation for his next phone call and the day she would meet Dave face-to-face.

Gillian's days flew by. She was busy at work, managing the loan Scott Sanders was granted for his dive shop, having her Friday lunch mastermind partners and hanging out with Sylvester. One of Sylvester's distant cousins and schoolmates, Julian Grainger, had moved back to Robertsville. Julian bought the property next door to Gillian. He was a strikingly handsome man of average height, a little bit chubby, with short brown hair and hazel eyes. When he smiled there was a little mischief in his eyes. He loved being back home in the area, found comfort living amongst old friends and family, and as a writer, he felt he had the perfect peaceful writing retreat. Julian's home was relatively small but had fifty acres of hardwood trees behind it. The little house was efficient and comfortable with a wraparound screened porch where Julian could write outside practically year round.

As it turned out, Gillian and Julian were kindred spirits. Julian became a mastermind partner at the Friday lunches with Sylvester and occasionally Scott joined them as well. Gillian was happy to have these gay men as friends and interested parties in her new adventures of dating online.

A couple of weeks after Julian moved next door, one morning as Gillian was having her coffee on her front porch, she watched him do something that looked like Yoga. Julian had a very specific daily routine. The third Sunday after Julian became her neighbor, Gillian invited him over for brunch to welcome him to the neighborhood. After a few mimosas, Gillian asked him what it was that he did on his front lawn every morning. Julian was happy to explain the way he started each day and why.

As he demystified his activity, Gillian learned about an ancient Chinese health care philosophy incorporating physical postures, breathing techniques, and focused intentions. Julian practiced Qigong every morning on his front lawn to start his day with focus. He'd watch the sun rise, feel the changes in the warmth of the air and breathe in fresh, clean, pure energy from the Earth and the sky.

Gillian was fascinated with the movements and as they became good neighbors and friends, Julian taught Gillian the practice of Qigong. Every morning at 6:00 a.m., they met under a century oak tree between their properties for their standing meditation, breath work and healing movements. Gillian had never been able to meditate with what she was told she had, a "monkey mind" that jumped all over the place. By learning about Qigong in general, the breath work and the actual exercises, Gillian was able to shift herself into her practice instantaneously and reach the full benefits of meditation. It reminded her of a Star Trek character, Seven of Nine, who was part Borg and part Human. At night, Seven of Nine would step into her alcove facing out. As soon as she was in place and plugged in, her eyes closed and her body was recharged. And that's how Gillian felt as she shifted into grounding herself to the Earth and beginning her practice.

Qigong was a good fit for Gillian, she could do it alone, with Julian, inside or outside, anywhere she could stretch out her arms, and not much space was required. And having a buddy to practice with made the entire process more enjoyable and increased the energy surrounding two rather than one. In fact, over time and with experience, Gillian enjoyed adding some Qigong movements into her belly dancing. The more she added, the more energy she felt. The more she practiced, the easier it became to move the energy throughout her body. She felt as if she was entering into a new world of spirituality. Gillian got to a point where she could feel the energy coming out of her left hand when she opened her palm to the sky. Although this level of spirituality was quite foreign to her, it was a gentle learning experience and it felt great. The more she danced; a new form of movement was created. At first she called it Effortless Energy Dance, and then changed it to Dance With Qi, which was belly dancing and Qigong combined. Over time, Gillian had taken belly dance classes with over seventy-five teachers in all styles from many countries. She had never had a class like the one she was developing for herself.

During the third week of speaking to Dave while he was in West Africa, Gillian's impression of their relationship was a fifty-fifty proposition that it was not real, after all, how could Dave be so in love with her when they had never met face-to-face? She was enjoying the attention, and it took her mind off her disappointment over her past two relationships with Will and Duke. Dave called Gillian every day for the next couple of weeks. It seemed they were getting closer and Gillian felt herself leaning towards falling in love. How could she imagine being in love with Dave without ever kissing him? When Dave called one morning, very depressed that his funds for the construction job had not come, he asked if Gillian would be able to cover his payroll. She responded that no, she would not. The call ended shortly after that with Dave's disappointment. That's when Gillian went online and did a reverse phone number look-up. From there, she paid for an online background check for more information. It turned out that Dave was actually a twenty-six year old Middle Eastern man named Khan who lived in Alexandria, Virginia. OMG! Gillian was surprised but not completely.

Gillian went online and wrote to "Dave" (not Dave) and revealed what her research provided. She even had his physical address. In her last email, Gillian asked Dave whose picture it was she had been staring at for the past month. She really wanted to meet that man! Dave never communicated again and Gillian learned a valuable lesson. She would research anyone she was interested in before having any kind of emotional connection, and pay a small fee to find out if they were real, it was worth it, reminding herself that information is power.

Gillian's phone rang late one Friday night. Her secretary, Diane, was scheduled to return to work the following Monday. Diane was upset and wanted to tell Gillian what was going on with her new man. Ultimately it turned out that Diane's beau, Marv, was a serial dater, and while she thought they were exclusive, they were not. On her trip home that weekend from Montana, while waiting for her connection and checking her emails on her laptop, she received a message from an online dating subscriber, even though she had changed her status to "it's complicated". She answered the message saying she was involved and thanked him for his message. Just for fun, she went back to Marv's profile and found him "active" and "single", looking for love. She felt a sinking feeling in her stomach. With plenty of time before her connection, she called Marv and asked him if he was he still pursuing a meeting for a new love on the dating site? Marv got defensive, made excuses and hung up rather abruptly. Diane figured out that she got her answer. Marv was also too good to be true.

Slowly, in a daze, Diane put her laptop back into the case, got out of her seat, got her carryon bag and went to the nearest bar in her airport terminal. She felt that a drink was in order as she digested what had just happened. Diane was very disappointed and disillusioned. She had herself a pity party for about a half an hour while waiting for her connection. After she finished her drink, she really needed to talk to someone so she called her boss and friend, Gillian. Gillian just listened. She heard the hurt in Diane's voice and wanted to comfort her. She told Diane about Dave and they shared their respective disappointments with each other. They both felt better and Gillian pointed out the fun Diane had been having over the past few months. The enjoyment, travel and entertainment she experienced during her relationship with Marv had been pleasurable, until this surprising ending.

Diane had never found the kind of love or sex Gillian had found repeatedly in her lifetime. Gillian was lucky that way. She experienced more relationships, interludes, affairs, encounters and more sex than most men ever did and now, even though Dave was not real, she was excited to have the freedom to explore more of them. The online dating site proved to be very entertaining. Gillian was getting messages from men of all ages, some of them boys as young as nineteen. She wondered why such young men would approach her. Gillian went to her profile one evening to read her messages and review what she had said the night she put her profile up. She was getting an average of twenty messages a day. She had to laugh out loud when she saw the box she checked by accident saying she was bisexual. Not believing she was truly bisexual, she unchecked that box and checked straight instead.

The next morning, it was noticeable that the

number of messages she was receiving was cut in half! Apparently, many of the men on that site were looking for the opportunity to experience a threesome, a *ménage-a-trois*. The messages continued for another week before Gillian found someone interesting enough to actually meet in person. Still, she was getting about ten messages a day from a variety of ages. Going back to her profile, she unchecked the box called casual sex. Within a few days, the number of messages Gillian received was again cut in half. She was fascinated by the entire process and to learn what some men are really looking for on the dating sites. Perhaps things outside their comfort zone that they did not know how to approach or express in person. Anonymity has its perks. Men and women could use any name, say anything they wanted, true or false, without ever being identified.

CHAPTER FOUR

Condoms

Friday's weekly lunch and mastermind with Sylvester and Scott proved beneficial for Gillian. Both of her friends had experience with online dating and when they found out Gillian was going to give online dating a try they felt it was time to have a conversation with her about protection. Sexually transmitted disease and infections were something to consider when engaging in casual sex or a chance meeting. Gillian wasn't really interested in meeting "the one" after Will and Duke. All she wanted and needed was sexual satisfaction to fulfill her personal need for expressing her sensuality. Sex was also Gillian's favorite way to exercise.

The following day, Gillian went to Tallahassee to one of the local drugstores. Robertsville was a small town and Gillian wanted to keep her personal life out of the town gossip. She walked inside and approached a young woman working in the store. Gillian asked her about her experience with condoms and the woman didn't know much more than Gillian. Together they looked at all the condoms. There was a good variety of lubricated, ribbed, grooved and latex condoms. As Gillian and the drugstore employee looked at all the packages, laughing along the way, Gillian asked about the sizes. What size should she get? A collaborative decision was made between the two women to buy small, medium and large condoms.

Would large condoms be enough, or did Gillian need magnum-sized condoms, too? There really was so much to consider! As their shopping adventure continued both women noticed there are no small condoms and realized why. What man would want to classify himself as small? The choice to buy assorted condoms and a lubricant was made after about twenty minutes of reading labels and trying to figure it all out. The young saleswoman and Gillian had had a fun time laughing and learning together. Gillian had never had any trouble connecting with people, even when the topic at hand would embarrass some folks. She thanked the saleswoman and headed back to Robertsville, ready for anything.

While Gillian never liked condoms, she thought Sylvester and Scott were right to recommend using them and she appreciated their concern. They told her to use them at least the first few times she encountered a new man, until she got to know him better. And recommended she learn each man's basic nature and how many others he was intimate with concurrently. Gillian believed that sleeping with a man was the easiest, quickest way to get to know the kind of person he was. Was he a gentle man? Was he a generous man with his time and his efforts? Was he a reciprocal lover? Or was he selfish, demanding or resistant to making sure you were satisfied? You could learn more about a man in two hours of sex than in a month. Why waste time? Being a bottom-line kind of person, Gillian would like to know right away if the new man had any potential in becoming a good friend and lover.

At a young age, Gillian realized that most people, including her parents, disagreed with her perception of lovemaking. Her mother told her it was important to make the man take her to dinner at least. If he didn't, it was a sign he was using her. Gillian's remark was that she was using him, so where was the necessity to spend money if what they both wanted was consensual physical and sexual satisfaction?

As an empathic child, Gillian felt warm sensations throughout her body and did not understand them. Her sensuality developed quite early and before she knew how to control the sensations she received from others, she began to enjoy them. Once she started having sex, she opened herself to receive the energy of others without knowing their impact. They felt good. When she finally got together with the person, it was time spent being totally vulnerable to her feelings. It was one of the rare times she was totally in the moment. She responded to the feelings of her body, her spirit, her need to feel connected and her need to satisfy those natural, unrestrained, unreasoned responses to the drive inside her. She followed her desire to reach the ultimate ecstatic release she found during sex. Gillian was certain that the wonderful feeling she had after sex was one of the things that kept her young looking.

When Gillian was seventeen, her little sister found her birth control pills in her drawer while she was snooping around. The pills made their way to their mother, and then, their father. On a Sunday breakfast with their dad in his apartment, Gillian's father sent her two sisters into the bedroom to watch television. He wanted to have "the talk" with his middle daughter in the kitchen. Her dad, Harry, asked her to not have sex again until after her eighteenth birthday. He asked her to promise him. Gillian said no. He asked a second time. Gillian said no; she didn't want to lie to him.

Quite disturbingly, Harry said that if Gillian didn't stop having sex, she was nothing more than a word that started with a C, had four letters, and ended with a T. Gillian's angry response was that if she were a boy, they would not even be having that conversation. Harry stopped talking because Gillian was right. It was not the best day for Gillian. Her sister betrayed her, her mother betrayed her and now, her dad was cussing her out. All because she was a free spirit and believed if a boy her age was allowed sexual freedom, she too was allowed the same freedom. Even if the larger population did not agree with her philosophy.

CHAPTER FIVE

Meet the Men

Shelley

Gillian's first real online date was with a fifty-eight year old man named Shelley. His profile described him as a man who enjoyed the outdoors, theatre, movies, music, cuddling on the couch watching television and cooking. He had a great job, loved living in Florida and was good at making his mate feel special. Chivalry was not dead. A woman should message him if they wanted to meet an honest fun guy who would treat them with the respect they deserved. His photograph was in front of water. He had silver hair, a beard and moustache, and was wearing sunglasses.

Shelley's first message to her was: Hi, drinks? After reading Gillian's profile, he was ready to meet. Being bored and somewhat lonely, Gillian agreed to meet him the next evening in Tallahassee at a lovely rooftop bar.

She was excited at the prospect of meeting a new sexy man and having some fun. The anticipation of getting ready for her date put a smile on her face as she showered, put on some red lace panties and bra, chose a spaghetti-strapped red top (Shelley's favorite color) and blue jeans, long dangling red glass earrings and a ruby heart pendant necklace. It was a warm evening so Gillian put her hair up in a ponytail with a red clip. After a quick check in the mirror, she put on a little make-up, found the perfect shade of coral lipstick and jumped into her car.

The drive was about forty-five minutes to the hotel bar; Gillian had her sunroof open and sang out loud all the way there. It was easy to recognize Shelley from his photograph. He was shorter and stockier than expected. And there was no mistaking Gillian; she only used recent photographs on her profile. They ordered vodka martinis and took them outside to look over the city of Tallahassee, watching the lights go on after the sunset. It was a beautiful night. Conversation came easily; they both had a sense of humor and got along. After their second martini, Shelley expressed his desire to be intimate with Gillian. Sitting on the comfortable loveseat cushions, leaning up against each other, feeling the warmth of the alcohol, the relaxation and arousal she felt after three hours with Shelley. He kissed her gently, three times, and she agreed to follow him home to his apartment in Tallahassee. Then he asked Gillian to let her hair down from the ponytail, as he really liked long hair. When she did, she enjoyed the way Shelley gently moved her hair away from her face. She felt her body come alive. Her sensuality was definitely out, her filters gone.

It was a short ride to Shelley's. His apartment was clean and well decorated. He put some music on, went into the kitchen and fixed them another drink of vodka. And he brought out a joint. It had been a while since Gillian smoked weed and the alcohol made it so her judgment may have been skewed. She happily joined Shelley smoking some weed. It was some very strong weed. After a couple of hits, Gillian had had enough. She relaxed into the music, listening to the nuances of the different instruments and asked Shelley to slow dance with her. They danced and danced into the night. The slow dancing was romantic and erotic, especially when Gillian noticed something pressing up against her jeans. It had been a long time since she had been intimate with a man. She grabbed his butt and pulled him closer to her pelvis to send a very clear message. They danced their way into his candlelit bedroom; the music still playing rhythm and blues, and Shelley ever so slowly undressed Gillian. Gillian had packed a condom in her jeans pocket earlier, just in case. She grabbed the condom and tossed it onto the nightstand as inconspicuously as possible.

First, Shelley undid her belt, then unzipped her jeans and pulled them down slowly. She had to steady herself on his shoulder as she delicately lifted her feet out of the jeans legs. Her red top came off easily over her head. When he got to her red lingerie he felt happy that she had paid attention to his favorite color. Her bra was a demi bra that covered about half of her breasts while lifting up a bit, and her panties were bikini style and all lace. He told Gillian that she was beautiful and so sexy. Gillian was there in the moment. Her brain wasn't working, but her body was working overtime. As her panties came off slowly, her arousal was evident. She was feeling yummy again.

Shelley took his time with Gillian, moving

his gentle, warm hands slowly up and down her body, laying her down on the bed. He kissed her from head to toe; he lingered at the back of her neck sending chills down her spine. She was enjoying the attention she had been missing. When Gillian was ready for Shelley to be inside her, he put his attentions and his mouth between her thighs. He started by exhaling warm air and then slowly put his lips on her body and gently sucked and kissed her. She exploded into orgasm in moments. He continued to eat her until she exploded again, and then turned himself around into the sixty-nine position. Gillian took his hardness into her mouth just as slowly and gently as he did for her. His moans of pleasure told Gillian that this was what he liked. Before he got too close to orgasm, he turned himself around again, face-to-face with Gillian, and kissed her deeply. He put the condom on and penetrated her slowly. Gillian found herself reaching up to kiss him while he was on top of her. Gillian exploded again and was mesmerized by the pleasure she was feeling without having been pounded into. Shelley was a very gentle, very experienced lover.

Gillian was too relaxed, too drunk and too

tired for the long ride home so Shelley made her stay overnight. It was a weekend so there was no rush in the morning, except to let her dogs outside. Gillian was awake listening to the birds at five-thirty in the morning. She woke up feeling refreshed and really appreciated Shelley's concern and hospitality. She enjoyed sleeping next to someone again. She decided that Shelley was an okay guy. Until a week later, when Shelley admitted he had a long-term, long distance relationship and didn't want to get involved. He only wanted a Friend with Benefits relationship. While Gillian enjoyed their one-night stand, she didn't think she wanted this particular man for that particular relationship, she did not want to be his booty call.

Danny

The next man Gillian met was Danny. Danny was forty-nine, lived in Tallahassee, and was a radio personality with his own show. He described himself as a decent looking, smart, creative, fun and romantic man that was awesome at sex and could cook. All that sounded good to Gillian. Danny had a beautiful smile, no facial hair, and a shaved head. He wrote well and had good punctuation and syntax. Having been an English major in high school, Gillian expected clear communication. She'd seen too many messages where "I" was not capitalized and the wrong tense was used or common words misspelled. It annoyed her. It was a sign that the person was an imposter, like Dave. Not Dave.

One of Danny's messages asked if Gillian gave massages. Danny thought it was amazing to get a massage from someone with good energy and to have the energy exchange. Since Gillian started doing Qigong with Julian she was more aware of energy than ever. Yes, she could give a massage. Danny liked giving massages as much as he liked getting them. They would get along splendidly. After writing online messages through the dating site for about a week, they exchanged phone numbers and Danny called to make a date. He suggested a little bar in Market Square in Tallahassee. Even though she asked, Danny never did tell Gillian his favorite color.

Gillian dressed up in black jeans, black high-heeled sandals, and a lacey black sleeveless top and of course, black lace lingerie underneath her clothes. She stuffed a couple of condoms into her back pocket too. Gillian left her naturally curly, strawberry blond hair down allowing it to flow down over her shoulders. It was a humid Friday night. If she dried and straightened her hair, it would just curl right back up. On her way out the door, she grabbed a bright silk scarf to add a little color to the black, sexy outfit she chose to meet Danny in. He sounded like such a cool guy. The bar he chose was on the north side of Tallahassee and it was a shorter drive for Gillian so she jumped into her car, half an hour before their meeting time. They arrived in the parking lot at the same time, recognized each other immediately and hugged hello before entering the bar. Danny was wearing a lavender long-sleeved shirt that complemented his very dark skin. He had the most beautiful smile.

Taking their seats at a tall table, they ordered a couple of extra-dry vodka martinis. Danny knew the owners of the bar, and one of them came over to meet Gillian and see how Danny was doing as he delivered their martinis. It was a nice introduction and Gillian felt special. A toast was made and the martinis were delicious. It was easy to talk to Danny; he was well spoken and knew a lot about energy exchanges. They sat across from each other and Danny asked if Gillian could feel his energy. Yes. Then he reached his hands, palms up, across the table and asked Gillian to hover her hands over his, palms down. Since energy comes in and out of our hands, there would be energy between them. And there was a tremendous heat between their hands, like electricity. It sent a surge of energy through Gillian and she could only imagine what it would be like to sleep with Danny. Or not sleep. Danny encouraged Gillian into her second martini and flirted incessantly with her. She must have smiled for two hours. She could feel herself opening up and becoming vulnerable to Danny.

When Danny invited Gillian home so he could cook her dinner, she said yes. Danny paid the check, walked Gillian to her car and told her to follow him home. There was something assertive about Danny. She almost liked being told what to do. The ride to Danny's was short as he said it would be. Danny was a typical bachelor, messy house, not much furniture, except two full bedrooms of furniture and a dining table covered in papers. He fixed them both a vodka drink with ice, and rummaged around in his kitchen pantry looking for

43

something to cook for dinner. The choice of linguine and clams was mutually decided upon as the perfect dinner. Danny wasn't kidding when he said he was a great cook. The pasta was perfect and he used just the right amount of garlic.

Danny was the perfect gentleman. He didn't jump on Gillian, he didn't grab her to kiss her or impose his stocky body on her slender frame. He gave her enough time to be comfortable, and had some food in her stomach to absorb some of the alcohol she'd been drinking. They talked on his couch for over an hour before he asked if he could kiss her. Gillian gave him permission and was surprised when he gave her a Tantric kiss, slow, soft and gentle. His tongue was soft and his kisses were sweet. Danny asked Gillian if she would mind taking off her clothes in the living room while he watched. Nope, she didn't mind. She did feel a little self-conscious but knew how good she looked and removed her outer clothing first. She let Danny look at her in her black lace lingerie for a moment and could see he was pleased. He asked her to leave her lingerie on and come into the bedroom.

Into the bedroom they went, Danny had already put a glass of ice water by the bed for

Gillian, a very sweet gesture. There was no blanket on the bed, only freshly ironed light green sheets. A jasmine candle was burning, the lighting was soft and Danny thought Gillian looked fabulous and very sexy. She had pulled the condoms out of her jeans pocket and put them on the dresser. He asked her to stand beside the bed. He came up behind her and wrapped his long, muscular arms around her entire body and held her. She felt an amazing surge of energy coming from his body, surrounding hers; it was different from anything she'd felt before. He unhooked her bra and slid her panties down and asked her to sit on the edge of the bed. He kneeled down in front of her, spread her legs and slid his middle finger inside her. He was tall enough to kiss her right where she was. As Danny kissed Gillian and moved his finger side to side, stroking her G spot, Gillian was more and more aroused. He quickly got her to orgasm, continuously kissing her. She loved what he was doing to her body.

Danny withdrew his finger, drew it to his lips to taste her, then dried his hand off on a nearby towel, and stood before Gillian so she could see what she did to him. He was hard as a rock with a little bit of cum at the tip of his dick.

Gillian took him into her mouth, tasted him, and gave him head until he made her stop. Gillian loved giving head and had been told she was quite good at it. She supposed she was. He told Gillian to stand up.

Danny sat on the edge of the bed and told Gillian to put his condom on, climb up onto his lap and straddle him. He slowly inched himself inside her as she lowered her body to his. Ouch. The condom and his size called for some extra lubrication. Danny used edible lubrication, something new to Gillian. That way they could go back and forth between oral sex and fucking. Gillian loved to learn new things. And experience different men. Danny made love to Gillian for two hours. He was a generous lover, making sure Gillian was satisfied, repeatedly. Gillian enjoyed the way Danny told her exactly what he wanted her to do. He even had her pretend her hands were tied above her head, not allowing her to touch him. It was very erotic and exciting. When they were finished and exhausted, they lay side-by-side, holding hands. Danny was saying how much he liked Gillian's energy, and as he said that, she felt his electric wave of energy surround her again. Was this something new? It was definitely something delightful and fulfilling. It was like being in a pool of love.

Their next date was just as much fun. Danny offered to give Gillian a massage on his massage table in his apartment. So the following weekend, Gillian drove down to Tallahassee to get her massage. Danny was an amazing massage therapist. He had strong hands with soft skin; he stayed connected to her body as he moved around the massage table. The room was warm, no lights were on but you could see if your eyes were open. Gillian's eyes were closed most of the time. She was becoming one with the table she was so relaxed. Danny reminded her to breathe deeply as he pressed harder on her lower spine and hips. Gillian had been belly dancing at home a lot and thought she may have pulled a hip muscle. Her muscles were so tight, and he knew she was tight inside as well as outside. Danny laughed to himself, out loud, and had to explain why. He made Gillian laugh and relax again after the deep tissue massage she ultimately got to help release her hip muscle. The oil Danny used for Gillian's massage was coconut oil. It had a light, sweet fragrance and melted on her skin. His hands moved slowly, continuously and effortlessly across her skin.

The delightful way Danny ended her massage was a first. Gillian's friends in California would refer to it as a happy ending. Danny told Gillian to bring her hips down to the edge of the massage table, allowing her knees to bend and legs to dangle over the edge. She complied. He stood between her legs and teased her with his erection. Then he sat on his massage stool and put his face between her thighs and started eating her. The sensations he gave her in addition to the relaxed state he had put her in were incredible. She couldn't move, which was okay because he told her not to move. Danny slid his finger inside Gillian as he continued to eat her, sliding it side-to-side until she could not hold still any longer and let out a scream of pleasure. Danny went back to teasing Gillian with his erection, which was even bigger than before, and he already had a condom on. Gillian drew up her torso from the massage table to take his face in her hands and kiss him. She held onto his neck as she lowered herself back down to the table and accepted his body inside hers. The warmth of Danny on top of her, the relaxed state she was in, and her mind clear and seeing and feeling only what was in front of her made Gillian feel like a million dollars. No, wait. A billion dollars!

It was moments like this in life that really made Gillian feel alive. She was always happy in general, grateful for the amazingly cool life she lived in the most beautiful place on the planet, but these moments were special. The men she chose responded to her sensuality and empathic nature and allowed her to see into their essence. What did they want? What did they really need? Gillian did her best to give it to them intuitively. In Danny's case, she knew he needed to give pleasure.

Gillian and Danny got together a couple more times. She reciprocated with a wonderful massage, including a happy ending. They talked more and more about sexual fantasies, and when Danny finally told Gillian what he really, really wanted, she could not go there. He got really drunk one night on the phone and confessed. He wanted her to humiliate him and slap him across the face as hard as she could during sex. As much as she enjoyed spending time with Danny, she was pushed away by the thought of him needing to be humiliated while enjoying sex. No, she couldn't go for the dichotomy of pleasure and violence. That was the end of that.

No More Martinis

After her first two rendezvous, Gillian decided not to drink any more martinis when she was first meeting with a new fella. She saw a pattern evolving and thought it best to slow down a little. As an empath, she was pretty good at gauging people and their intentions. But, despite her search for pleasure and sexual satisfaction, she made a promise to herself that she would not sleep with a man the first time they met, even though she may be having great fun.

Bob

Bob chose Gillian on the dating site and clicked the button that says, "I want to meet you." After receiving a notification, she read his profile. He was tall, blue eyed and mostly bald. He had lived on the Hare Krishna commune in California and Hawaii in his early years. He was an Internet guru now. He lived in Tallahassee and loved the beach. That was great for Gillian; she was due for a visit to the beach. They agreed to meet at Mashes Sands Beach in Panacea on a Saturday morning at 11:00.

Bob wore a khaki fishing hat and looked kind of cute for a sixty-year-old man. He was slender, very intelligent and had a good vibe about him. Bob had a gentle soul kind of vibe. Gillian liked him right away and felt safe. They hung out for a couple of hours and decided to meet again the following weekend. Bob was into dancing and drumming and asked Gillian to come over for a Jacuzzi and give him a dance lesson. She thought it was an unusual request but knew male belly dancers so she said yes.

Gillian arrived at Bob's Tallahassee home just after noon one Saturday. Bob brought out towels for the Jacuzzi and a joint. His fenced backyard was landscaped beautifully; it was a sunshiny, warm day. They talked and casually disrobed, then got into the warm, bubbling water, both of them pleased with the appearance of the other. They smoked pot and talked for an hour. They had both been to Big Sur backpacking in the late seventies. It was a comfortable conversation and at the end, Bob leaned in towards Gillian to kiss her. She enjoyed the feel of his lips and taste of his tongue. They sat naked in garden chairs to dry off in the sunshine. It was a naturally good feeling. It reminded Gillian of the nude beaches north of Malibu. Zuma Beach was the nude beach she used to visit on a regular basis. She loved the feeling of the sun caressing her entire body. The heat between her thighs was so intense it was pleasurable.

Once dry, they went back inside and Gillian put on her dance leotard and a hip scarf with coins. Bob put on some Middle Eastern music and they started their dance lesson. Bob really just wanted to see Gillian dance, he wasn't that interested in participating. The lesson didn't last more than thirty minutes and that was enough for Bob. He was mesmerized by Gillian and the way she moved - slowly, sensually and confidently with grace.

Realizing they were both hungry, Gillian asked what she could make for lunch. They had discussed food before her visit; Bob was a vegetarian so Gillian brought fresh salad greens, parsley, tomatoes and cucumbers from her garden, with pine nuts and walnuts. Bob found some mushrooms and bell peppers in his fridge and they had a lovely salad outside by the Jacuzzi under the covered patio.

After lunch, they had a toast with a shot of

Lebanese liquor that was one hundred proof. It tasted like licorice and packed a wallop, and was a great breath freshener. They went into the living room, sat on the couch and watched a nature show on television. Bob had his arm around Gillian's neck and started massaging her neck. She loved it. If she were a cat, she would have been purring. He held her close and kissed her again and asked if she would like to make love. She said she would. He told her he'd be right back. Bob went to take a pill to enable him to maintain an erection.

They snuggled again on the couch, Bob ran his fingers softly through Gillian's hair, and minutes later, poof, there it was. For the next four hours, Gillian and Bob had sex in multiple positions, in multiple spots around the house, in the yard, in the Jacuzzi, on the floor, in front of the television, watching porno because Bob could not orgasm. They stopped for another snack and went back to it. With each hour, Bob became less gentle in his lovemaking. After four hours of being pounded into, Gillian could take no more. While she regretted the fact that she had so many orgasms and he had none, she needed to leave because he was getting way too forceful for her body to accept anymore. She was sore all the way home and was so very happy to see her sweet dogs and go crash in her own bed that night.

Bob called again for another date a few days later. Gillian thought it was best to not go back there again. As nice as Bob was, the sex with him was not fun and satisfying, it was difficult and four hours was just too much. She remembered how he had her on a bed, pinned up against the wall while he pounded into her. It wasn't anything as enjoyable as Shelley or Danny. They were gentle and made love. Bob just wanted to fuck the s**t out of someone. Bob didn't give up. He continued to invite Gillian to the beach or to a sinkhole to swim but Gillian didn't trust him to not hurt her again.

The Crazy Man

This fella wrote to Gillian, "Scorpios are fun together!" And it was true; she knew being with another Scorpio would be a memorable experience for sure. They wrote for over a week through the dating site, exchanged phone numbers and started talking. His name was Jim, he was fifty, short, built like a gymnast, clean shaven, and had very short gray hair, dark olive skin and green eyes. He lived on the north side of Tallahassee, was from the Miami area and was headed back there for a family reunion. Their meeting would have to wait until he got back.

Over the next week, Jim texted, called and sent Gillian pictures, of his family, being out on a boat, always in front of the water. Gillian longed for a trip to the beach and put it in the back of her mind to go the next weekend. She was pleased that he took the time to communicate with her while he was on vacation with his family. When he came home a week later, they made arrangements to meet at a fine dining restaurant on Apalachee Parkway. They both arrived on time and sat in the bar for cocktails. They were instantly attracted to each other. They had one drink before deciding to go grab a sandwich at Jim's favorite Cuban restaurant. After dinner, they sat in Jim's car and smoked a joint. They agreed that they would see each other again and then Jim walked Gillian to her car.

Gillian thought it was kind of strange when Jim insisted she kiss him in the parking lot. They shared a brief kiss on the lips. Jim asked Gillian to text him when she got home to let him know she arrived safely. Gillian promised to text. When she got home, as she undressed, she remembered to text Jim about her being home. She texted, "Home safe, had a great time! Looking forward to seeing you again." About ten minutes later, her phone rang. It was Jim. He was yelling at her. He said, "What kind of text is this? You couldn't pick up the phone and call me?"

Gillian was in shock at this reaction. She complied with his request and he was screaming at her. She told him she that she didn't think it was going to work between them, and that she didn't care for his attitude and was going to hang up. She hung up. Jim called back several times and she ignored the ringing of her cell phone, happy that she had not given him her home phone number. Once Jim realized she would not speak to him, he started texting her, repeatedly. She read the texts but did not respond. He was apologizing, telling her that he really wanted to see her again. Gillian already knew she would never see this crazy man again. For the next three months, Jim continued to text, call and send her messages through the dating site. Gillian responded only once to his email messages saying she was not interested and to please stop contacting her.

Millie's L.A. Adventure

One Sunday afternoon, Gillian's friend, Millie called to check in. Millie was a Head Hunter in Los Angeles and the friend that suggested Gillian's current position as Robertsville Savings and Loan President as a fresh start. Millie was delighted to hear how much Gillian was enjoying her new life, beautiful new home, new career and her fresh new interest in online dating. They shared stories about their experiences in meeting men online, laughing harder with each story. Millie had been online dating for a few years, and had met several men for short and long-term relationships. She remained friends with about half of them because they were okay guys, but yet "the one" for her.

Gillian was not looking for "the one", just some fun with a regular sex partner. She was still hurt over the last time she fell in love. She was in no hurry to go there again. Gillian didn't spend too much time rehashing her experience with Will to Millie but wanted to mention him because it was such an intense interlude. And that's about all it had been regardless of how Gillian felt about Will. It was going to be difficult to find someone she would find so irresistible again. And it was disappointing that Duke would have been that man, if he could only keep his mouth shut. No, Gillian didn't need anything serious until she was free from residual feelings for Will.

Millie saved the best story for last. She met Adam online, after a few days of email messages; they exchanged cell phone numbers and hit it off really well during their first call. A week later they decided to meet for a drink at a bar on Wilshire Boulevard. Millie parked across the street from the bar, walked to the signal, crossed the street and found Adam at the front door, just as good looking as his profile photograph. She gave a sigh of relief, as there were times the men did not look nearly as good as their photographs. Adam was tall, handsome and a gentleman. He held the door for Millie, guided her to a table and held her seat out for her. They were enjoying their first meeting in person, talking about where they had travelled, what kind of music they enjoyed, their favorite foods. Millie was having a great time. And then, Adam reached his hands out across the table, to take Millie's hands, and said, "You are so gorgeous, I just want to reach across the table and kiss you!"

Millie was a bit more reserved than he was and was glad he didn't actually lean across the table to kiss her. They ordered steamed oyster appetizers with capers and Parmesan cheese, onion rings and chicken wings. Chicken wings were such a sexy food to eat. It was a sweet and savory meal. They finished their dinner and Adam, even though he was parked in front of the bar, walked Millie across the street to her car. He gently kissed her goodnight and said goodbye. Millie waited in her car for ten minutes because she was going in the same direction as Adam but didn't want him to see her make a U-turn and have it appear that she was following him. She checked her cell for messages and emails before starting her drive home.

By the time Millie got on the road, right ahead of her at the signal were flashing lights and she heard an ambulance coming from behind her. She stopped and pulled off the road to learn that a car had hit Adam as he walked across the street in the crosswalk. He was dazed and covered in blood and saw Millie. He asked her to take his wallet and car keys and follow the ambulance to the hospital. She was stunned and did as he asked. They weren't far from the hospital, Adam was taken to triage and found out his hip was broken.

After the nurses got Adam settled in a room, Millie, although not a relative, was allowed to visit for a few minutes because he kept asking for her. Apparently Adam was so taken with Millie, he did not pay attention when he walked across the street. It was dark, he was in dark clothing, and the driver never saw him. Millie sat with Adam after his x-rays were taken and waited for his son to get there. She didn't feel right about leaving him alone since she felt it was because of her that a car hit him. It truly was not her fault but she really felt badly.

About two months later, Adam called Millie. He was on his way to recovery, still doing physical therapy. His son had stayed with him and he was getting around okay. Adam told Millie that as much as he liked her, as sexy as she was, as beautiful as she was, every time he looked at her he would remember being hit by a car and he did not want to see her again. That was fine with Millie; she thought he was a little too clingy for her. Millie would always feel badly about what happened after their date and that's no way to start a relationship. She thanked Adam for calling and said she understood and wished him well.

CHAPTER SIX

Glenn

Gillian did not give up on her quest to meet a regular lover and continued searching online for a suitable partner. The online dating service sent her a message saying she had become someone's favorite. A tall, dark skinned, fifty year old, shaved head, brown eyes, wore glasses and had a southern accent. He had been raised south of Tallahassee in Summerland and now lived in Shell Point Beach in a relatively new condominium. He could see the Gulf of Mexico from his front windows. The sunsets were magnificent and it sounded so romantic to Gillian. She wanted to meet Glenn right away. Her fear of meeting strangers was gone but she paid attention to everything. She always met them in public and never gave her last name, home phone number or address until she was sure she wanted them in her life.

Glenn was a stock option trader and had as much free time as he wanted, he had learned the Holy Grail of stock trading options and futures and had done very well. He had spent the last few months travelling through Italy while visiting his mother, buying clothes and tapestries, had pictures to share and stories to tell. He was intelligent and sensitive and Gillian had a good feeling about this man. Glenn was friendly and talkative and he was a Scorpio. She loved Scorpio men, except for the crazy one earlier in the year. When they decided to meet, Gillian asked if they could meet at Lake Talquin for a picnic as their first meeting. She was tired of meeting her dates for a drink. She wanted to get to know Glenn in a more casual setting. He thought it was a great idea and they chose to meet the following Saturday.

A conversation ensued about food for their picnic. Glenn was an omnivore like Gillian, stayed away from fried foods, loved vegetables and was good with any food. He offered to pick up sandwiches but Gillian said she would rather make them in the park and asked Glenn to bring some sliced oven-roasted turkey and whatever sandwich rolls he liked. She had some avocados that were perfect for use. Glenn said he'd found a lovely Sauvignon Blanc wine when he was in Italy and had brought a case home. He said he would bring a bottle to their picnic on the lake.

Saturday morning Gillian found her large wicker picnic basket, her red and white checkered picnic blanket, red cloth napkins, pink plastic plates, a small cutting board, a couple of knives, some silverware, plastic glasses and plastic wine goblets. Gillian grabbed the Spike from her spice cabinet; some cucumbers, celery and greens from her garden; a couple of bottles of spring water; and a small container of mayonnaise. She put some ice from the freezer into zip lock bags. Instead of chips, she had lightly steamed some asparagus for something crunchy. She packed a small container of Greek salad dressing for a dip, some sliced baby Swiss cheese, and a small ripe seedless watermelon. Then Gillian jumped into the shower, dried her hair straight and put it in a ponytail giving her a youthful appearance. She put on her sunscreen and a lightweight, lavender cotton top with spaghetti straps and decided not to wear a bra. She did select some pretty panties and a pair of stretch jean leggings and beige sandals; she would be sitting on the ground on a blanket and wanted to be comfortable.

Gillian was driving a red mini-SUV and was

easy to spot in the parking lot at Lake Talquin State Forest. Glenn approached her car and she admired his tall, muscular body. He looked just like his photograph online, uniquely good looking. Both of them smiled from ear to ear as they saw each other for the first time. She felt the familiar Scorpio connection and instant attraction. Gillian saw a gleam in his eyes and could tell he liked the way she looked. They had a quick hug, the energy exchange was good and they decided to drive over to one of the primitive campgrounds for a private little space for their picnic. They found the perfect spot, unloaded the food and picnic basket from their vehicles. Glenn had brought a great big thick blanket for the ground and there was a handy picnic table available for the preparation of lunch. All the food was put onto the table and Gillian got to work making their sandwiches while Glenn talked with her. He watched her slice the cucumbers and celery; she looked so graceful and feminine. He liked her look, the way she dressed, the way she smelled and the way she smiled at him. He liked the sparkle in her dark brown eyes. He was already enjoying himself with Gillian.

Gillian took the rolls Glenn brought, put

mayonnaise on the top and mashed half an avocado on the bottom of each, then sprinkled Spike on both sides. She placed the turkey on top of the avocado, then a slice of Swiss cheese, thinly sliced cucumbers, some greens and then the top of the roll. Glenn was impressed with Gillian's creativity and appreciated the healthy sides of celery and asparagus with Greek salad dressing. It was nutritious and delicious. Glenn uncorked the wine and poured it into the plastic goblets and made them both some ice water too. It was sexy watching Gillian eat the crunchy asparagus and celery, she was deliberate as she slowly bit a small piece and chewed it slowly, looking deep into his eyes. He could just imagine how her tongue was moving the food around her mouth. What was she thinking about? Glenn found Gillian very sensuous and Gillian found Glenn just gorgeous. All she could do was smile. And think about their next date. Did she really have to wait for a second date to experience him?

After lunch they took a walk down a nature trail for about an hour. The wine mellowed them out and they walked slowly; the sound of the river was constant and calming. Glenn had the softest, deepest voice, easy enough to hear and very seductive. He could talk about anything; he'd had an adventurous life and was a great storyteller. Glenn told Gillian about another dating site he had been on where the women were mostly college students and needed financial support. There were some young women that were bold enough to ask for money just to meet him, and then to state the weekly allowance they expected. Gillian laughed her head off as he continued his story and used an acronym "GPS". "What's GPS?" she asked. She almost fell down laughing when he explained the concept of Golden Pussy Syndrome, as these women, really girls, thought of themselves deserving to be paid a high fee just to visit with the men. Glenn had the means and could have had any number of these young women, as good-looking as he was, and he chose Gillian. He said it was because the younger women had nothing to talk about, no life experiences, no snappy conversations and no depth.

Gillian really liked Glenn and was glad to spend time in nature with him; they had that affinity in common. Being outdoors in the fresh air, their inner children came out to play with each other. They talked about anything and everything. Glenn was well educated and fascinating to listen to. Gillian was entertaining, intelligent and outgoing. The picnic was a good idea. They had been in the park for four hours and Gillian did not want their date to end. She felt safe with Glenn and decided to invite him home with her. She was happy when she saw his face light up, as he didn't want their date to end either. He agreed to follow her home and spend some more time with her. After seeing how easily Gillian prepared a delicious meal, he thought that if he was lucky, maybe she would cook him dinner.

And Glenn was in luck. It was early evening when they arrived at Gillian's. Her dogs were very happy to see her and greeted Glenn with their friendly natures. He loved dogs and her dogs loved him. It was a good indicator. Gillian gave him a tour of her gardens and her home and they settled down on the front porch to watch the sun finally set. The jasmine was blooming and fragrance was in the air. The evening became warm and balmy and made them a little sleepy after a day in the sunshine. They let the dogs run around for a half hour. Gillian offered a shot of sipping tequila to Glenn, which he readily accepted. He also was fond of tequila and liked the same kind.

Gillian had not expected to be serving dinner for anyone and had not gone shopping. While in her garden, they harvested some collard greens, purple cabbage leaves, Swiss chard and green onions. She snipped some fresh thyme and parsley and when they got back inside, she took some bacon out of the freezer and stuck it in the microwave to defrost. Gillian liked to cook her bacon in the oven on a baking sheet covered in tin foil. It was so easy to clean up and no splatter all over the stove. As the bacon cooked, Gillian sautéed a green pepper, an onion and a whole clove of garlic in a large saucepan in a little bit of coconut oil. She added a little chicken broth and a couple of pieces of bacon from the oven, after breaking the bacon up. She turned the heat down and covered the saucepan while she chopped up the collard greens, Swiss chard and green onions. She then added that to the saucepan and put the lid back on. Ten minutes before serving, Gillian added the freshly harvested thyme and parsley for a light peppery flavor and delicious aroma.

One of Gillian's favorite foods was a roasted chicken from the local grocery store. They really came in handy for dinners, sandwiches, chicken salad and chicken on a salad. Luckily she had a whole one in her fridge, she bought one every week. Glenn offered to pour them another shot of tequila while she cooked. He was right there beside her in the kitchen helping the whole time. Whether it was washing a dish or chopping garlic or simply entertaining Gillian while she worked. It was a lot of fun and very casual. It felt like they were really getting to know each other.

Glenn thought Gillian looked really cute in her kitchen apron. It was purple with a beautiful dragonfly on the front and when Gillian tied it around her waist, it accented her shapely body. Glenn sighed; Gillian even looked good working in the kitchen. She was so graceful. He remembered from her profile that she was a belly dancer, and had been dancing her whole life. She actually moved like a dancer. The soft jazz music playing in the living room made Glenn want to pull her close and dance with her in the kitchen.

It wasn't long before dinner was ready. Roasted chicken, greens and another bottle of the Italian wine Glenn had brought. Dinner was sweet and savory. The watermelon came home with them from their picnic so they had that for dessert. It turned out to be a very sexy dessert. Gillian served thick slices of watermelon and as they ate it, the juices dripped down their hands and they laughed like children. This was turning out to be quite the first date. Their attraction to each other was right on. Their conversations were interesting and they made each other laugh easily. Things were looking good after those two shots of tequila and a bottle of wine with dinner.

Rather than turn on the television, Gillian took Glenn back outside to the porch and invited him to sit on the loveseat swing with her. He took his seat beside her; close enough to put his arm around her shoulder. She was warm and soft and still smelled good. He gently massaged her neck and shoulders, and she felt herself relaxing into his arms, enjoying his touch. When he kissed her for the first time, it was wonderful. He approached her slowly, initiating the kiss with a bit of Tantra, holding off before making contact and barely using his tongue other than to brush her upper lip lightly with it. Gillian was hungry for more. It had been a while since she had been intimate with anyone. The men she had been meeting lately were just not her cup of tea.

Glenn shared his desire about wanting to get physical with Gillian. After he kissed her a few times she was ready and excused herself for a moment. After a long day in the sun, she wanted to freshen up. The panties she'd been wearing were kind of wet from hanging out with Glenn for so long, and she wanted to taste really good for him. She wanted this to be more than a one-night stand. Gillian took the fastest shower of her life, dried off quickly, spritzed her fragrance on and put a tight, stretchy blue print mini-dress on. After a quick check in the mirror, she was ready to go see Glenn for some romance and she went back outside commando style. She had let her hair down from the ponytail, and it was soft and still straight. Gillian thought of this as romance, but what she really wanted was to enjoy her body and her sensuality.

Not wanting to broadcast their activities to her new neighbor, Julian, Gillian took Glenn by the hand into her bedroom. She helped him unbuckle his pants and asked him to sit on the chair beside her bed. Feeling rather uninhibited, Gillian straddled Glenn and sat in his lap face-to-face with him. She gently put her lips on his and kissed him the way he had kissed her on the porch. It was a slow, delicate kiss. Gillian used the tip of her tongue to trace the outline of Glenn's full lips. When she completed the circle, Glenn opened his mouth and gave her a really deep kiss. They both noticed what had come up and out of Glenn's unbuckled pants.

This excited Gillian tremendously, she was happy with what she saw and how her body was reacting; she felt so warmly aroused and alive. She told him to stay where he was as she slid down to the floor in front of the chair and took him into her mouth. Tequila had that effect on her; her oral fixation was stronger when she drank it. Gillian kissed and caressed Glenn as she performed oral sex. She would come up for air and gently kiss him on his beautiful lips. After a few kisses, she would go back to work in pleasuring Glenn. It had gotten dark and even with Gillian's curtains open, all they could see of each other was their silhouette. The darkness improved their sense of touch. Each contact became more enticing. Glenn could take no more and took Gillian by the shoulders, moved her away from the chair, stood up and whisked Gillian around and put her in the chair before she could react.

The little blue mini-dress Gillian was wearing was hiked up around her waist by the time she hit the chair. It was easy access to her ready and willing body and Glenn approached her like an expert. He tickled her with one of his fingers gently, slid another finger inside her wetness and lowered his head to her body. Gillian was in heaven. This new man instinctively knew what she needed, wanted and loved. Glenn took his time with her as she had taken her time with him. Gillian got to the peak of orgasm several times but didn't quite make it over the edge. She had some hesitation about being on her chair and making a mess. She reached down to Glenn's head, with her fingers under his chin; she brought his face to hers and kissed him.

"Take me to bed," Gillian whispered. Glenn stood up, lifted Gillian out of her chair and put her on the bed. He lay next to her and turned her on her side to face him. They stayed together like that, holding each other, breathing in each other's essence for a few minutes. They had just met, the connection was strong and it felt as if they already knew each other. Glenn slid inside Gillian very slowly. Her body was ready but it was still their first time. He didn't want to hurt her with his generous size. As soon as Glenn was inside Gillian she exploded in orgasm. And she kept exploding until he did too. They both realized this first time was making love, not just having sex. It was very satisfying to them both. It was as if they both really needed that. Glenn stayed for another hour, cuddling with Gillian and kissed her on the mouth, on the cheek and on the top of her head as they said goodbye for the night. That was the best online date Gillian had ever had.

CHAPTER SEVEN

Shell Point Beach

Sunday morning Glenn called Gillian before noon. He expressed his enjoyment of their first meeting and said it felt more familiar to him than the very first time being with someone. Gillian credited herself for being an empath, and recognized Glenn's ability to make such sweet love to her, and how he knew just what to do. Glenn didn't know what an empath was so Gillian explained and directed him to a website before they concluded their call. Once he read about thirty traits of an empath he learned he had over half of them. Now he understood his "knowing", an ability to feel what needs to be done, staying calm in a crisis. He'd always had that gift. Gillian had twenty-eight out of thirty traits. Sometimes she thought it was a gift, other times, a curse. To be so sensitive to everyone, emotionally, energetically, and physically - was not an easy thing to experience on a daily basis.

The worst trait, Gillian thought, was being hurt easily. There was a trace of hurt left over from Will. There were days she would just cry because he left such a void in her life. Regardless of her original anger over the way she thought he disrespected her, her heart ached for him - until recently, since she had met Glenn. Gillian knew her heart would be guarded with Glenn. She wasn't ready for another heartbreak. Just being comfortable with casual sex, understanding the Friends with Benefits arrangement, Gillian could see herself with Glenn in a long-term relationship. And knowing these things ahead of time was one of her capabilities.

Gillian found living out in the country was quiet. She couldn't hear and feel anyone, just see the cows, horses, goats and sheep she passed and waved to on her way to work. She had never been so happy driving to work before. She was surrounded by nature until she hit the main street in Robertsville. And even then, the quaint little country town had its own pace. No one was in a hurry; the energy was soft instead of chaotic. Friendly people greeted you on the streets; it was a nice place to live. Glenn had that open, friendly demeanor about him. Gillian felt calm with him; there were no anxious energies about him.

Monday morning Gillian arrived at work with a big smile on her face. Her secretary, Diane, noticed immediately and said, "You look radiant! Spill!" Diane followed Gillian into her office and closed the door. In as few words as possible, Gillian gave Diane a quick rundown of her first date with Glenn. Gillian was grateful to have Diane's friendship and someone to share some of the more personal things with. Diane was happy for Gillian and said she was not going to give up on online dating yet.

Right before noon, Glenn called Gillian on her cell phone. He asked if she was free for lunch. She agreed to meet him at the Boxwood Bar and Grill for lunch in fifteen minutes. That would give her five minutes to get ready and ten to drive there. Happy that she had chosen to wear a lovely white linen dress with bright colorful flowers and red high heels to work, she dabbed some of her favorite oil on her wrists, put some lip color on and fluffed up her hair. Glenn was waiting in the parking lot and a great big smile came across his face as she drove in. He was a striking man in his light blue shirt and jeans. The color was complementary to his skin.

They greeted each other as friends with a big hug and went inside to order lunch. Gillian ordered her usual at the Boxwood, a cheeseburger all the way. Glenn took Gillian's recommendation and ordered the same. They walked out to the backyard to look for seats at one of the picnic tables. It was a gorgeous day, too humid for straight hair and her hair was becoming curly. Glenn noticed a difference from over the weekend; he liked it curly. Her hair was soft and bouncy and it shined like gold in the sunshine as they walked to their seats at the table under an umbrella.

Before their cheeseburgers were served, Glenn invited Gillian to his condo for the weekend. Gillian was thrilled at the thought of spending the weekend at the beach, watching the sunset, drinking her coffee at the beach. Yes. She'd be happy to join him. When she got back to work, she asked Diane if she was available to pet sit for her. Yes, she was. It was settled. Gillian had something to look forward to all week. During her lunch breaks she thought about what to wear, what to cook, what to bring. In no time, it was Friday and she was having one of her usual mastermind lunches with Sylvester, Scott and Julian and was happy to share her excitement with them. Julian offered to keep an eye on her home and said he looked forward to meeting Diane.

Saturday was another beautiful day. It wasn't summer yet and being in the sun was still tolerable. Gillian's overnight bag was packed and ready to go before she showered. She was so excited; she found a joint someone had left at her house and took a hit to calm herself down. No tequila drinking during the daytimes; it was one of her rules. Gillian shaved her legs, put some oil on her skin before lightly drying off and chose an orange crocheted bikini. She'd already packed her black bikini and flowered tankini. The jeans shorts and orange cotton top were waiting on the chair by her bed. Gillian had just bought a pair of espadrilles with a wedge heel that she decided to wear, and she brought an extra pair of flat sandals. She was ready by ten o'clock, which meant she would be at the beach in an hour. She couldn't wait.

Gillian texted Glenn to say she was on her way, and asked if she needed to pick anything up? No. Then she texted Diane to say the house was all hers until Sunday evening, if all went well. The route to the beach was through the

Apalachicola National Forest and was delightful. Gillian enjoyed the ride through a corridor of trees. She had her sunroof open, the sun shined down on her head and shoulders, her nervous excitement subsided and she felt at peace. Her navigation system directed her to Glenn's condo; there was a parking space at the bottom of his steps. He anticipated her arrival and was outside watering his container garden landscaping. There were bright red geraniums, orange marigolds, elephant ears and lilies, quite the assortment. Each plant had its own shape and size and color, all of the containers were either a copper or turquoise color. One turquoise vase, turned on its side, was a small decorative fountain. Gillian liked it all. It was unique, like Glenn.

She grabbed the overnight bag out of her car, and smiled a big smile at Glenn. He could feel her excitement, and they ran upstairs inside to set her bag down. Glenn had two glasses ready for mimosas on his kitchen counter. While he made them, Gillian stripped off her jeans and top, kicked off her shoes, and ran down the front steps to the beach like a child. Glenn laughed as he followed her there with the mimosas and a couple of towels. The tide was out, the beach looked bigger than usual. Glenn found a great spot and put their towels down on the sand. He toasted "To us!" and they kissed after their first sip. Gillian set her glass down in the sand and threw her arms around Glenn's neck, she felt deliriously happy. She kissed his sweet lips lightly. Their connection was definitely there and very strong.

Glenn had done his shopping. He had eggplant, zucchini, yellow squash, mushrooms, onions and garlic. After noon, they went inside and roasted the vegetables tossed in some olive oil, salt and pepper. Gillian appreciated the fact that Glenn was a healthy eater. While the veggies were in the oven, they sat on his balcony with another mimosa enjoying the view and their time together. Glenn regaled Gillian with stories of Robertsville in the early days when Coca Cola stock was being offered and the number of millionaires that lived in her area. She was fascinated. He was so intelligent. She loved listening to his melodic voice, the way he spoke was a pleasure to hear. Any tension Gillian felt prior to her arrival was gone. All she wanted was to feel his arms around her again, holding her tight, making her feel special.

Once the veggies were fully roasted, Glenn pulled out pre-made pizza dough from his fridge, some mozzarella cheese, Parmesan cheese and green onions. He spread the dough on the pizza pan, drizzled some olive oil and added a layer of cheese, then the roasted veggies, and then more cheese and topped the pizza with sliced green onions. The pizza was great and after lunch, they went back to their towels on the beach for a nap. Gillian had brought a little book for some light reading so when she woke up from her nap and Glenn was still sleeping, she read for an hour. The sound of the surf, the sun shining on them, and this beautiful, sweet man lying next to her. Gillian longed for nothing other than what was right in front of her.

Towards early evening, Glenn woke up groggy from the mimosas, went inside and woke himself up with a shower. He invited Gillian to take a shower with him. He had the coolest shower Gillian had ever seen. There were two separate showerheads at different ends of the large glass tiled shower. They could leisurely shower together. After a little while, Glenn became erect watching Gillian lather up her beautiful body. He didn't try to hide it, as that would have been difficult. He approached her from behind and walked her to the wall of the shower, kissing her neck as they moved forward. He spread her feet apart with his and gently slid inside her from behind. She relaxed into his body as he penetrated her. Glenn was so yummy. His touch so gentle, so sweet, Gillian was allowing her sensuality to come out unfettered. After their release they dried each other off, put some clothes on and went back to the balcony.

Glenn made filet mignon, roasted potatoes and a salad for dinner. It was to-die-for delicious. Gillian wasn't used to a man cooking for her and she just loved a home-cooked meal, especially if she didn't have to cook it. Glenn was going to spoil her. He could do anything, including satisfy her physical needs.

Gillian loved the way that Glenn held the back of her head as he moved inside her. She loved that, when he was on top and she opened her eyes, he was always looking into her eyes. The eyes are the windows to the soul. Gillian had her most powerful orgasms, looking into Glenn's dark brown eyes; she felt that he saw into her soul. She could feel that there was a very deep connection and vague past life impressions that made each experience with Glenn that much more intense.

Fascinated with the sexual and sensual satisfaction Gillian found with Glenn, with time, the intensity, satisfaction and desire surprisingly increased for her as well. Gillian decided Glenn was the best lover all around that she had ever had, and there had been enough lovers to make a very educated decision. It was more than his ability; it was his willingness and desire to please her that she admired and appreciated.

He was special in the sense of reciprocity; Gillian enjoyed giving head, and was always willing and creative. Much of Gillian's pleasure came from when Glenn would go down on her. His technique was always good but, as he learned more and more about Gillian's body, he became extremely creative with his mouth, lips and tongue. Glenn made Gillian ejaculate so much that they always had a towel nearby to put beneath them. It pleased Glenn that he was able to give so much pleasure to a woman, a woman like Gillian. She was a hard-working professional, and President of a local bank. He was impressed with her intelligence as well as her beautiful body, and the way she knew how to please a man. In particular, Glenn admired Gillian for her ability to release herself into ecstatic sensual pleasure.

More and more often Gillian was interested in making love with Glenn. When they were together they would give each other that Scorpio look of intensity and both knew what was soon to be felt, the pleasure, the release, and the happy vibes when they were done. It was becoming a ritual, day or night. After work, and a cocktail, winding down from her day while playing with her two wonderful dogs on her lawn, Gillian looked forward to feeling Glenn's hands and lips on her body. Because Glenn was a stock trader, he worked anytime he felt like it and took time off anytime he felt like it. He was available to Gillian and didn't mind the beautiful drive up to Robertsville.

There was a tequila kind of ritual. If Glenn saw Gillian drinking tequila, he knew she would be most interested in satisfying her oral fixation by sucking on him. Just the thought of her lips wrapped gently around him, the flow of the movement of her mouth around his shaft and head made him hard. He would take his very large, very hard dick out of his pants, showing Gillian his arousal. It was barely moments before he was in her mouth and she was enjoying his taste. For some reason, tequila allowed Gillian to ignore the cum that was being deposited into her mouth, she swallowed it gladly.

One particular day after seeing Gillian drink a shot of sipping tequila, Glenn stood proudly in front of Gillian and said, "You owe me head." Gillian asked Glenn to wait in the living room until she showered and promised him thirty minutes of head, even though she didn't understand why she would "owe" him head. After she showered, she put on a dark green lace dress, without the black sheath dress it came with as a slip, and showed off her beautiful body. Gillian directed Glenn to sit on a large circular cushion chair and sat in front of him on a small red leather cube. There was soulful rhythm and blues music in the background, the lights were dimmed, candles lit and the ceiling fans were going.

Gillian slowly took a seat in front of Glenn and took him into her mouth as he relaxed on the cushion. She kept her word and gave him head for more than thirty minutes. He was delicious, his skin a dark chocolate brown color, and with his fresh clean smell - all made for a very sensuous experience. Glenn was pleased that Gillian wasn't kidding about the thirty minutes and when she was done, he took her into the bedroom, laid her on the bed, felt her wetness and slid his long, hard, beautiful dick inside her. Once accustomed to his size, Gillian was able to relax and feel the tip of Glenn penetrating her so deeply it made her cry out. He had figured out a way to reach her G-spot by going deep inside her and staying there until she ejaculated around him. He loved when she did that and no lubrication was required, even after an hour, if he continued to stop moving every once in a while and allowed her to explode with pleasure. He could always tell because Gillian held her breath as she experienced and enjoyed an orgasm. When she finished, she was always gasping for her breath.

Over time, Gillian invited Glenn to join her in her Qigong practice with Julian. He learned to enjoy the meditative quality and it felt great. If he spent the night at Gillian's he would do it with them before she went off to work and he headed back to his condo on Shell Point Beach. They worked on their breath work using an open-mouthed breathing technique, and they both noticed their lung capacity increase. They also noticed that if they used the open-mouthed breathing during their lovemaking, it increased their pleasure exponentially. Gillian had no idea sex could bring her to a spiritual level she had never reached before.

CHAPTER EIGHT

The After Dinner Mint

One evening Glenn came over with a bag of small candy bars. They were made of chocolate and a cracker, and had a mint filling. They were delicious! Glenn offered Gillian a bite just before jumping into bed. She took a small bite and really enjoyed the feeling of chocolate melting in her mouth, the crunch of the cracker and the strong minty flavor. As Glenn approached Gillian with romantic intentions, he gave her another bite of chocolate. Gillian's senses were alive with pleasure. Her sense for touch was filled with the intensity of Glenn's large muscular body, his soft skin and gentle tongue.

Gillian's taste sensations were on fire. Glenn would kiss Gillian between bites as she herself melted into his arms and allowed him to penetrate her. She was completely distracted from the usual gasp of air every time he went inside her. Gillian loved the way Glenn held her head the whole time he made love to her. It was a rare intimacy. She loved the energy coming from the warmth of his hands as if she was enveloped by his love. She loved the way she came with all her might as she held onto his strong body. This time Glenn hugged her just as tightly and Gillian felt a shift in something.

Letting her guard down a little, Gillian brought up a conversation about where their relationship was going. Glenn told her about an upcoming trip. His mother, living in Italy, was ill and had been given six months to live without treatment. At eighty-five, after living a full life of love and adventure, his mom decided to opt out of the painful treatment for her disease and die a natural death, with her son by her side. He would be leaving in less than a month. He wanted Gillian to know how much he enjoyed their time together and how fond of her he was. He would miss her and did not expect her to wait on him. She was free to do what she wanted in his absence. Well, that was fine but Gillian would really miss Glenn. A little disappointed, Gillian accepted that he was leaving and at least he was honest about it and released her from any implied commitment to him.

The last few weeks before Glenn left were intensely physical; they both wanted to get as much of each other as they could before his departure. Gillian was sore by the time he left. Knowing how much Gillian loved being at the water, Glenn gave her a set of keys to his condo. He told her to use it as often as she liked, for whatever she wanted to use it for. It would be great to have someone checking on it every so often.

CHAPTER NINE

Meet Ali

Before leaving for Italy, Glenn had basically given Gillian permission to have an affair or do whatever she wanted to with whomever she chose. Not that she needed his permission, but she thought he was being considerate. And perhaps, it was his way of saying that he would indulge given the opportunity. Gillian couldn't imagine being with another man just yet, Glenn being the best lover she'd had ever had. Glenn would call her when the time was right for both of them. She told him that she didn't want to look for another man but she was feeling a physical need that he used to fill. Gillian jokingly told him she should just find herself a woman. Glenn is excited by the whole idea and has fun as he hears about her new experimental goal. For a forty-seven year old woman, Gillian was pretty and hot. She had this sensual aura about her along with a childlike innocence. She was all that and a professional too. Gillian could hold her cool in the boardroom and be a seductress in the bedroom. He would like to be a fly on the wall and watch it all he thought to himself.

Even though Gillian belly danced a few times a week for exercise, to help her release some of her extra energy, she decided to join the Robertsville local gym. It was one of those anytime gyms, where you could go at your preferred hours. There were always different people there and Gillian made some new friends. One day, Gillian rushed across the parking lot, dragging her gym bag behind her, determined to get a great work out this day. Work was so absorbing that she really had to take time away from the office to kick off those high heels and sweat for a while to keep up her health and her body. On this particular morning, with a meeting cancelled, Gillian had the perfect opportunity to sneak out for a couple of hours. Always having a gym bag and a set of workout clothing in her trunk made anytime a good time to go. And as she rushed across the parking lot, she felt someone's eyes upon her. Perusing the area, she recognized the source.

It was a woman, a small but built, short, dark-haired, olive-skinned beauty. Gillian took a second look thinking she looked like a man; in fact, she thought she was looking at a cute guy at first. The woman was smiling at her. Gillian watched as this woman looked at her from top to bottom and lingering at her thighs when she finished. This excited Gillian more than she would have allowed a few years back. In her early thirties Gillian admitted to herself that she must be bisexual. Why else would she get creamy when she saw a woman who was kind of butch, and think to herself "Now that's a cute guy!" Missing Glenn and feeling a bit lonely, she hungered for a little companionship. She slowed her walking down and steered toward towards the attractive woman, separating her lips with a smile.

"Good morning! Isn't it a beautiful day? Are you a member at this gym? I'm Ali, what's your name?" she asked. "I'm Gillian, I've been coming to this gym for a few months and I don't believe I've ever seen you." Ali answered, "I'm new in town and thought I'd join the gym and make some new friends." Gillian sighed with relief and the thought that her loneliness might be quite temporary. Ali and Gillian entered the gym together and then the locker room to change. Gillian carefully removed her suit, hung it up in her locker and changed into her sports bra, black unitard, socks and sneakers and looked really cute and svelte. Ali unabashedly shed her jeans and sweatshirt and donned her shorts and t-shirt, socks and sneakers. She looked cute too in a boyish kind of way. Gillian could see her shapely, tan legs and a chill went down her spine.

First they jumped on the treadmills, then the stair masters, while they kept up some light conversation about the weather and the neighborhood and they built up a sweat. As they went their separate ways, Gillian hummed Marvin Gaye's "Let's Get It On" to herself and walked over to the passive weights. Ali went to the hand held macho weights and continued her workout. There were plenty of guys surrounding the dumbbells as Ali got into her workout. The men in the gym were happy to give her advice, they suggested new techniques, and they were very friendly fellas. Ali thought to herself that this was a nice place to have moved and happy that she found a nice new job in a nice new town.

Ali worked as a technical support person for a major billing company that serviced many different companies. She could transfer anywhere they had an office when she needed a change of scenery. It was a great indoor job, no heavy lifting, lots of new people to speak to every day, and no real supervision. As long as she showed up and did her job, the boss left her alone. There were always great stories to tell about her crazy customers and she had a new one every day. After Ali's breakup with her last partner, she needed a change. They broke up six months before Ali's fortieth birthday. Everything reminded her of her ex-girlfriend, her apartment, her job (especially since her ex-girlfriend still worked in her old department), and her old stomping grounds. Since her life revolved around "their" friends, there was no escape other than to move away. And if she was going to move, she wanted to experience living in another state.

Now that Ali had gotten her feet wet in this new place, so to speak, her anxiety was starting to melt away and she turned her thoughts back to her new friend, Gillian. She wondered if Gillian was still in the gym. Looking around and to the opposite end of the room, she found

Gillian gently dabbing her face with a towel. She walked over to Gillian and said, "Looks like you're about done with your workout for the day!" "Yes! And I feel great! I'm so glad I came today!" said Gillian. Ali asked, "I've worked up quite an appetite. How about some lunch?" Gillian pouted as she responded, "Oh, I've got to get back to work now, but why don't we meet for a drink at 6:00 this evening?" Ali responded, "Sounds great but you'll have to give me directions. Do you have a special place in mind?" Gillian told her about their quaint little neighborhood bar; Boxwood Bar and Grill, not far from the gym. Ali remembered seeing it on her way over and said that was fine.

They returned to the locker room for their showers, each of them glancing over to see each other's bodies as covertly as possible. Both girls smiled at what they saw and got ready to leave. They walked out to the parking lot together, gave each other a little hug goodbye. "See you at six!" They said simultaneously.

Gillian was aware of how her body felt warm after the embrace and hoped for more later. Gillian sang aloud all the way back to work with the radio blasting in her car, thinking, "Good thing the sunroof was closed today." All the way back, driving to her office she contemplated what to wear to her date tonight and how deep Ali might be willing to go in their budding friendship. Chills ran down her spine as she considered the possibilities. The afternoon sped by for Gillian. And for Ali too. Both women were imagining their date to be ideal and have a happy ending.

Gillian rushed home to change at five o'clock. Off went her suit and after a very quick, hot shower, she dried off and dusted herself with delicately perfumed powder. First Gillian put on her lovely gray lace matching lingerie, then she put on a peach-colored sparkling tank top underneath a gray, lacey woven long-sleeved top and a pair of tight blue jeans. Yes, she looked hot. She let her hair down from the clip and watched her long curls fall to her shoulders. I hope Ali likes my hair when it gets in her face later, Gillian thought, fairly confident of the night's end.

What Gillian didn't know yet, the thing about being with a woman, as opposed to a man, was the stronger emotional connection. Normally, it was not a one-night stand, but Gillian would be okay with that. She just really needed some attention. She craved the softness and nurturing nature of a woman for a change. Glenn was a wonderful lover and great friend but, sometimes, maybe a girl just needed to be with another girl to get that deep emotionally charged sex. Strangely enough, while Ali was getting ready she considered a similar thought. Ali wanted to be closer to Gillian. She wanted to feel the slow evolution and subtleties of their connection and see where it would go. After all it was Friday night and they had all weekend to explore each other, providing Gillian was in the same frame of mind.

Ali showered and changed into jeans, a black t-shirt and a black blazer. Yeah, that's good, Ali thought to herself. She looked trim and attractive. Her short dark hair was shiny and straight. Ali took a quick look at her watch and decided it was time to be on her way. She hopped in her car parked in front of her apartment and off she went to the Boxwood Bar and Grill. It wasn't far and Ali arrived at the same time as Gillian. They parked next to each other in the back lot and greeted each other with a gentle hug. They were alone in the dark; it was quiet and conducive to romance. The hug was filled with feeling and there was an exchange of energy that filled the senses. Ali was wearing a delicious man's cologne Gillian was familiar with and really liked. Gillian smelled sweet with her usual fragrance, felt wonderful, looked beautiful and her touch was electric. Ali thought she looked really hot in her tight blue jeans, and let her eyes settle on Gillian's breasts before looking into her eyes, her beautiful brown eyes.

Suddenly Ali felt very vulnerable. Gillian had swept her off her feet when they met at the gym; she noticed earlier that there was no wedding ring on Gillian's left hand. Is Gillian involved with someone? Then the thought crossed her mind. Is Gillian gay or bi-curious? Something Ali will ask about once they are seated for dinner. Ali had hoped for a friendship-first kind of relationship with Gillian. The physical sex with a woman was a bonus to the emotional sex. Women had a different way of approaching intimacy, and wholeness to a relationship was a reflection of women-energy. Women have such a different energy than men; it's what makes them so special.

The girls shared an anthropological discussion over dinner. Ali came from a long line of Native American healers that used ceremony, energy and plant-based medicines. She was quite intriguing and very attractive. Gillian talked about recently learning Qigong and the benefits she experienced practicing nearly every day. After a couple of glasses of wine, it seemed like they were playing footsies under the table while getting to know each other. They were at a small, cozy table and every time one of them moved her foot or crossed her legs, she would bump the other. There was nothing but smiles all through dinner. Gillian was enjoying the attention of this new friend.

Ali was sexy in a boyish kind of way. The longer they sat at their little table exchanging energy, building a bubble around them, the more Gillian wanted to lean over and kiss Ali. What she really wanted was for Ali to lean over the table and kiss her. Ali woke Gillian out of her fantasy by saying she was feeling a strong energy connection and asked Gillian if she was feeling it too. Yes. She was. Ali reached her hand out across the table as she stood up inviting Gillian to leave with her. Their tab had been paid and they were ready to go.

Next stop, Lake Talquin to look at the moon. It was Ali's suggestion and Gillian was flattered and feeling all kinds of new and some familiar feelings in her body being with this woman. Leaving Gillian's car at the Boxwood, Ali drove her to the lake; a gorgeous night with the sporty convertible top down made the whole thing enchanting to Gillian. The moon was full, and the sky full of stars. Gillian laid her seat back a little and watched the sky all the way to the lake.

Ali parked at the Lake Talquin State Park Lake Boardwalk. The moon was so bright it was easy to see as they walked out onto the boardwalk. The water was still and reflective. Looking out over the water, they talked for another hour, about how each of them got to Robertsville and what they were enjoying about it. Ali stood close to Gillian as she leaned on the railing, put her arm around her waist and pulled her closer. Gillian turned towards Ali allowing her to feel her lips. She thought, "What a sweet feeling it was to kiss a woman." Ali gently brushed her hand across one of Gillian's nipples sending tingles throughout her body and making her sigh with pleasure. They kissed in the moonlight until they reached the point of no return. Ali had such a gentle touch and Gillian wanted to feel more. She invited Ali to come home with her so they went back to Boxwood Bar and Grill, Gillian picked up her car and Ali followed her home.

Gillian called Ali's cell from her car and talked to her throughout their ride home. Ali thought that was a lovely gesture to make the drive go by quickly and to not lose the connection they established on their first date. She was really taken with Gillian, knew Gillian was attracted to her, and loved that Gillian was a good kisser. Gillian did not seem like her orientation was strictly to women. But, did that matter? If two women were attracted to each other, would it not be the same feeling of attraction as a woman and a man who were attracted to each other? They would just both be female. Or male.

Over dinner earlier, while talking about their families, Ali learned that Gillian was raised with a gay aunt and was not affected by antiquated cultural stereotypes created by the idea of homosexual sexual activity. Some had a preconceived notion that there would be a difference in the feelings of love due to gender. Was she feeling the early stages of love or lust for Gillian? It had been a long time since Ali had been intimate with anyone. She was ready, and after hearing about Gillian's escapades with other women, always at the request of the man in her life, Ali knew Gillian wasn't straight as a board, and she certainly was receptive to Ali's advances.

They arrived at Gillian's home; it was dark and Gillian needed to let her dogs out for a little while. The dogs greeted Gillian and Ali as they ran outside; Gillian invited Ali inside for a quick tour, ending in the kitchen. Gillian offered Ali a shot of sipping tequila, and Ali accepted. They took their drinks onto the porch while the dogs ran around the yard. It was too dark to show Ali her garden and Gillian wondered if Ali would be there in the morning so she could show her. Maybe Ali would have some ideas to add to Gillian's gardens. Gillian was already imagining a continuing relationship with Ali to her own surprise.

Ali found the loveseat swing on Gillian's porch and sat there, patting her hand down to signal Gillian to join her there. They were still sipping on their first shot of tequila. Ali got out her cell phone and put on some Internet radio, a soft, calm station. Once the dogs came back to the porch, the two women went inside. Ali connected her music to Gillian's speakers and continued setting the mood for a very pleasant evening. Ali reached out her hand to take Gillian's and asked her to slow dance in the living room. Ali was a little bit shorter than Gillian and it felt so good to be in her arms. Ali could put her head against Gillian's shoulder and Gillian could smell Ali's hair, feel the softness against her face. They were living in the moment, feeling what was between them, recognizing a knowing that they would be together physically soon. They were certainly off to a good start. Their bodies fit well together.

Ali took the lead, sitting Gillian on the couch then leaning in to kiss her, she gently pressed Gillian lower onto the couch so she was laying down. Ali got on top of her, all the while kissing her, leading her. She slid one hand into Gillian's tight jeans and managed to get to her sweet spot, and found that it was very wet. Ali's finger slid inside Gillian with ease. It was easy to read Gillian she was expressive and vocal. Ali knew just how to please her. Sitting up straight, she stayed on top of Gillian and slowly removed her gray shirt and then the peach sparkling cami to see a beautiful gray lace bra. It was so sexy and such a turn on for her; she kissed Gillian even more deeply than before.

Standing up, Ali watched Gillian as she removed her jeans. Gillian was breathing deeply, biting her bottom lip as she slithered out of those tight jeans. Then she lifted up off the couch just enough to help Ali out of her pants. Gillian didn't wait for Ali to lead again. She brought Ali's naked body towards her and kissed her pelvis gently, using the tip of her tongue to graze lightly over Ali's body. She noticed how skillfully Ali unhooked her bra and threw it to the side. Ali's hands were in the right place to fondle Gillian's breasts. Gillian moaned with pleasure as she kept kissing Ali's beautiful firm body.

"Let's go into the bedroom," said Gillian. And off they went for a night of sensual pleasures. Gillian had paid close attention when Glenn gave her head. He was an expert! The way his lips caressed her body, gently kissing, licking and sucking her most sensitive spots. Gillian was anxious to learn if she could please Ali in that same way. Gillian just got more excited thinking about how Ali would taste. After taking the rest of their lingerie off, they stood face-to-face beside the bed. This time Gillian leaned Ali onto the bed as they kissed.

Their tongues danced a slow, sensuous dance. Gillian slipped her finger into Ali's arousal as she had her tongue in Ali's mouth; she was so soft and so warm inside. Gillian decided this was more than a science experiment, like her other encounters with women when a man was present. This was cool. Her senses were alive and wondrous and hungry.

Before Gillian could slide herself down between Ali's legs to taste her, Ali's finger found its way back inside Gillian. Still kissing, totally engaged, totally in sync, they came simultaneously. Gillian did not let the momentary break keep her from what she wanted. When she took her finger out of Ali, she brought it up to her mouth and slowly sucked on her finger. Ali was delicious. Her breasts were lovely, her nipples erect, her belly flat. Gillian kissed her all the way down to the spot she craved. Using her knowledge of Tantric lovemaking, she barely touched Ali. She breathed her hot breath on Ali's waiting body. Then ever so lightly touched her with her soft tongue. She ran her tongue around slowly, occasionally across her clitoris. When she left her tongue right there, Ali would squirm and moan. Yes, Gillian could satisfy a woman, after all, she was one and knew what she liked best.

Gillian was in heaven making gentle love to Ali and having Ali respond to her in the same way. It was so easy, it was so natural and it was so tender and totally satisfying for them both. They drifted off to sleep until morning. When they woke up in each other's arms, they were smiling. Their hair a mess, the top sheet and blanket thrown on the floor, only panties on the floor, no clothing. Both early risers, they jumped up and went to the bathrooms meeting in the kitchen for coffee. Gillian gave Ali a short red silk robe to wear and put on a long black silk robe. There was an excitement in the air. Something new and beautiful was developing. They took their coffee out to the porch and saw Julian doing his morning Qigong ritual exercise at the old oak tree.

Not wanting to advertise to Julian in their robes, the girls kept their voices low but when they laughed about something, Julian turned and took note of their presence. He walked towards them smiling, understanding what was going on. Gillian introduced him to Ali and offered him a cup of coffee. Yes. Coffee would be nice. On the spur of the moment, Gillian asked Julian if he would be around over the weekend to keep an eye on her dogs, feed them dinner and let them out in the morning. Yes. He would. Julian would pet sit for as long as she needed him to. He loved Gillian's dogs and had become part of their family. Gillian gave Julian an extra house key before he left.

With all her responsibilities under control, Gillian invited Ali to spend the weekend at Glenn's Shell Point Beach condo. Ali was thrilled about spending time on the beach, something she had in common with Gillian. Yes. She would love to join her for the weekend. Ali dressed quickly and took off for home; she had to shower and pack for her next adventure. And Gillian's heart was pounding happily with expectations of her next escapade.

More Escapades of a Belly Dancer

Coming soon ~ In Volume Three, *A Weekend with Ali,* Gillian has an experiential relationship with another woman who recently moved to town. Gillian's love interest, Glenn, is out of the country and they share stories about their respective adventures until his return. Ali becomes part of their social circle and influences the way Gillian feels about her monogamous orientation.

www.YourPathwayToPleasure.com

www.BelleSouth.club